DRAW NEAR

By Betty L. Beer

Scurfpea
Publishing L.L.C.

First edition 2025.

Cover artwork: Detail from "A Tree Drops Its Leaves Too Soon"
        by Betty L. Beer.

Scurfpea Publishing LLC
P.O. Box 46
Sioux Falls, SD 57101
scurfpeapublishing.com
editor@scurfpeapublishing.com

Poems

Draw Near

Once on a spring day, I went
outside and found a stick for
drawing. I came prepared
with India ink and good,
supported paper. I looked
long at a tree and its branches.
I drew its hard winters and
drought years that gave
it a gesture of its own,
all its own.

Could

Gramps and I walked north after eating spaghetti
in the only restaurant open in Winona.
Two shiny rails planted in concrete, poured
in the Thirties, still without cracks, stopped us.

We looked left. "Hop on a train here", he said,
And you could go all the way to California."

Out of the blue, I saw my high school's U.S. wall map
scrolling down the wall, dingy Prussian blue, dull pink,
faded ochre, shaping Illinois and California, all the states.
I saw the Burlington Northern bumping its way
to the warm Pacific making a C against a Colorado
mountain, air likely tasting of minerals. I saw the engineer
waving to the brakeman in the caboose and the brakeman
waving back.

The Story of a Drawing

Having his portrait painted was something 83-year-old
Mr. Foster was about to scratch off his bucket list.
As he sits in his easy chair in front of his cluttered kitchen,
I take a long look at the topography of his lived life. I see
that he hides nothing, no masks, it's all there.
I take a deep breath and begin.

It's not enough to just draw what's in the light. That only gets
you the modern flat plane. Shadows make roundness –
the spheres of skull and eyeballs, the nose pyramid,
the complexity of ears. A little conté draws the fleshy pinkness
of his cheeks that contrasts with his smooth, pale forehead –
a farmer's forehead that was always shaded by a John Deere hat.
What once was chaos on the page now evolves into recognizable
parts. I add highlights to his cheeks, forehead, bald head,
and, lastly, Rembrandt's glint to his moistened lower lip.

Time moves when he tells me stories, but I'm unable to talk
much. Sometimes I'm so involved that I don't even hear
him – I'm "in the zone" – but only for about twenty minutes,
and then my body tells me to pause. Mr. Foster appreciates
it, too, because holding a pose is hard work.

Now we chat, and he tells me a funny story about eating
mountain oysters. I tell him one, too, about eating road kill
at Augie Busch's house when I was a young lawyer in St. Louis.
We both laugh, then get back to work.

The Wife's Rant

There it is again, one of those awful car
shows my husband turns on when he's
run out of energy to do anything else –
car porn I call it. Those shows are on
every time I walk into the living room.
I hate that their garage is cleaner
than my kitchen. I hate that their t-shirts
are color-coded with this week's car paint.
Here comes an old guy paying 20 times
the original purchase price for a perfect
replica of a car, complete with memories
that didn't happen to him. Then there's
that tall guy with an engineer's degree.
He's sure not color-coded. Only works
with rusty motors. He just loves them!
This guy gets his cars out of junkyards!
No back seat, pavement peeks through,
bumper hangs out. Look at that idiot!
Smoke pouring out the back and he's
wearing a gas mask! Giggling through
a stop sign! Makes me exhausted.

Weather

Driving through a South
Dakota whiteout, I see
a wastefulness of white.
Today an expansive landscape
of cool wimple white under
lavish, warm white sky,
yesterday a reversal:
warm golden land under
grey-blue cloud cover.
Each day I'm tucked between
these blankets that are
stitched together with
receding telephone poles.

Mississippi Flood Brings an Epiphany

A dam's roller opens, brown claws tumble
        powering solid anger downstream

where limbs reach and swirl and drown,
        joining sullen currents of helplessness.

Washing through our home, five filing
        cabinets of experience

float, leaking memory and place until
        the waters thin, ripple clean

revealing paths to wideness. Acceptance
        becomes a friend who shows us

the solace of letting go.

Cape Sounion is noted for its Temple of Poseidon, God of the Sea in classical mythology, one of the major monuments of the Golden Age of Athens. It was built on the headland, surrounded by the sea on three sides. Its sunsets are unforgettable. The ruins bear the deeply engraved name of English Romantic poet, Lord Byron (1788-1824) who was a gun runner for the Greeks in its War of Independence against the Ottoman Empire.

Climate Change

At dusty sundown on Sounion's temple,
red pillars rehouse flittering wings
that shadow Byron's carved signature.
This rock jutting out of turquoise water
once grew primal forests that calmed
Poseidon with scents of pine and cypress.

Inside a Small Plane
When It Meets a Small Cloud

A belligerence of whiteness
forces itself through tightly
closed eyes like a madness.

Light thicker than skin grabs
my body like red fingers over
a flashlight. I want to fight it.

I wonder if the pilot senses
my pulsing red glow, an
extravagance of throbbing energy.

I'm immobilized by brilliance
until we fly out of it, regaining
our wavelength of calm.

Plum Creek Myth

Side by side we leaned
over the bridge rail
below idle
clouds laid back in
bright blue beds

We each loved
the creek, watching
it amble through
the town like an
untroubled pooch
in summer

I taught him how
to play Pooh sticks
and as we dropped
our twigs then ran
from side to side
and waited for the
winner; he warned
me not to pick up
a turtle because if
he bites you he won't
let go until it rains

In a Courtyard: Kabul, Afghanistan

A tall pale-turbaned man
swings his fan-rake out of
a circular pool, flinging
droplets of water that arch
into the cool morning air.

Against the sun, they gleam
like spun petals of mica,
and, as they fall, they wash
the garden's air before
gently patting the ground.

He walks around his pool,
blossoming rain onto the dust,
his thin white robe a bleached
silhouette against shaded rock.

In a Spice Factory on the Island of Grenada

Six women sit in a large warehouse,
        dust motes winking across
the slatted sunlight. On that planked
        floor, straight-backed, legs
akimbo, each one sifts piles of
        aromatic spices, hand over
hand, plucking nut from blade.
        Ebony thumbs strum brown
nutmeg and its subtle sibling, red
        mace, whose hornlike, shiny
strands lace the seed. The air is
        warm with our memories of
hot-spiced drinks, savory meals
        and fresh doughnuts.
Five women are bare-headed.
        Gripping the head of the sixth
is a hat that tells us she's their boss. I
        wonder, where did that hat come
from – It is a '50's style, black velvet shell
        with a small, black, airy veil, a
Chanel look in the Caribbean, proclaiming
        authority better than any weapon.

Sounds of Mackinac Island,
    Called Big Turtle Island

Glottal stop of horses' hooves,
        rondos of egressive bilabial clicks,

fricatives of gulls' wings and
        pileated woodpecker chords,

T-tapps of eagle and crow,
        red squirrels' high recitatives,

together with a beating of drums call up
        Anishinaabe at Turtle Shell mound.

Skating Match

Frisking against the cold
like lambs, wool-wrapped
parents and kids flock
around the home-made rink,
alerted by the announcer's
red mittens tapping a beat.
The boys, age ten, are next
in the final match.
A whistle, then push-off,
and little Bobby Cooper
springs near the front
of the pack. Someone
in the crowd notices that
he'd forgotten to zip his jeans,
which becomes more obvious
the lower he gets into his stride.
Someone else starts to clap,
which drives him even lower as
he flies out front, the glint on his
zipper's metal teeth like a beacon.
His fly opening looms larger,
taking the shape of round,
shocked eyes and open jaws.
Now, over the sound of pounding
ice, the crowd howls, and as
little Bobby Cooper dashes first
over the finish line, (with only
Bobby and the announcer
ignorant of the real action),
the announcer shouts
"There goes a crowd pleaser!"

Shapeshifter

She plucks harp strings strong to hear the melody.
Sounds of *The Water Is Wide* pass through
her window and enter a fast wind-stream,
fluttering the leaves of a quaking aspen at Itasca
State Park, the origin of the Mighty Mississippi.

It's not so wide here at the headwaters, watching
fingers of water, ridged like corrugated cardboard,
slide over submerged rocks as the river leaves
the rain-swollen lake. The current is fast.
One large woman in black falls in, then crosses
stones on her hands and knees, her black hair
catching the current, then trailing down her back
as she carefully stands up.

Two little girls in pink splash each other, raining
giggles into the creek, their mother on the shore,
holding one girl's glasses. A dozen little boys cross
farther down, ignoring stepping stones,
ignoring goosebumps on their bare chests,
looking for turtles.

She remembers learning respect for the wide
waters of her childhood, far downstream, when she
saw the Mighty River flood and swallow, as deep
as deep can be, all the houses in the nearby river-town;
when she heard Girl Scouts reverently sing the song
over a camp fire, while families from four hundred
homes slowly rebuilt on the high bluff above the river.

Vision Quest

Bobby saw three circling bald eagles the evening
of his vision quest. They flew high in a spiral.
The spotted one, like all teens, flew higher.

He watched them until they vanished, and thought
of connection becoming disconnection, and thought
of experience becoming memory.

In the morning a mature eagle flew past his eyes
no higher than a flagpole, no longer graceful,
in such a hurry Bobby could hear him pant.

Calculating Angles

Calculating angles off the grey
walls battered by racquetballs,
the old man swings through his
routine. His shiny biceps, calves –
hard from youthful corn-picking
and a life castrating hogs and
de-horning calves – are heating up.
He whips the racquet against
his large fingers and fakes a groan
as two young men, both in their
prime, finding all the courts full,
ask "Hey, buddy, want a game?"
Later, leaving warm humidity and
echoing chirps, the old man
lifts his chin and lengthens
his stride to the outside as he
hears a disgusted young voice,
"Wiry old bastard, isn't he?"

If You Were Michelangelo

when you began to dream of David's form,

you'd ask which image was worth months

of marble dust sanding your clavicle, months

of your sinew opened by a chisel, months

of merging your own spark:

the victorious moment after Goliath's death,

or the chalky worry just before the sling?

All farmers know that the riskiest time for a wheat crop is after it is cut and before it's in a shelter, because an unexpected rain can rot the whole crop and a year's work is lost.

Neighbors, 1927

At midnight, after Old Mr. Shuler's plans
for a rich wheat harvest shattered
along with his left leg,
ten-year-old William and his friends
shove their giggles into their fists,
squeeze out of their screened
farmhouse windows, drop like seeds,
and blow into their neighbor's field.

All night their shadows bend, rake and pitch,
bringing in the crop with powered heaves,
and just before the lightning signals a
cloudburst, they hurl golden bundles into
his barn and run to their beds, their shoes
flinging a trail of yellow fines.

They dream that the old man looks out
his east window in dread of ruin,

And laughs, yes laughs at the rain.

Observation

I wish as a child someone would have
taken me aside and showed me how
to observe the behavior of my peers
and my family. It would have given
me a lot of insight, me surrounded by
fear and the rumpled ideas that
clothed those young years. I might
have learned how to make a friend,
instead of believing it was all about
how I performed.

It's simple, really, just look. Gestures
say a lot. Glances say a lot. I could have
watched facial expressions and listened
to spaces. I could have understood.

In every walk with nature
one receives far more
than he seeks. – John Muir

Receiving Far More

"Isn't it just gorgeous
out there", our son says,
his words shifting my gaze
from the pattern of gray
waves on Leech Lake
to the thin horizon
of green leaves
and winking windows,
to the pink sky that paints
itself into the mercury-like
waves. I'm glad he brings
me to this, with his laugh
that is like a giant walleye
springing up out of the lake.
He says it many times this week
and once even diverts me from
musing over an insipid
watercolor I painted
in high school that didn't win
a prize at the county fair,
and it becomes gorgeous
for me each day too.

Two Porches – Both Good Enough

Our front porch was wide, firm to the home,
white wooden rails on three sides and wide steps
to the ground. We played there in all seasons,
looking through its spindles, sitting on its shiny
grey planks and white top rails. The best days
were rainy days, listening to rhythms, light
on the roof, thunderous on the concrete,
making back-splashes that drove us to sit
close to the wall to watch rain-greyed homes
winking next door.

Bobby's porch was narrow with black metal steps
that bumped against the house. He didn't sit
there much because he had to move when family
walked up, their muddy shoes scraping on the
perforated steps. Once, he climbed up its stair rail
and it almost tipped over. His father started a wide
wood porch replacement, but only built a platform
without steps or rails. It puddled in summer rains,
overlooked green trees down a long hill that smelled
dirt-damp in spring. But it was good enough to jump
in any direction.

The Day I was Beckoned into a Watercolor

It was in Kabul that I was invited into a John Singer Sargent watercolor.
Oh, the man
was as handsome as that work of art, with cobalt-blue
eyes that pierced from jet black brows.

Not in Sargent's Bedouin blue, but wrapped in white, he was sitting on
white, surrounded
by white. "He wants to kiss you", his helper said. You can have
twenty-five percent off anything in the store down the street.

I stood there, curious, unafraid, surprised. He was bareheaded,
taller, surrounded by standing, curious, robed elders,
in tan Pashtun hats.

I paused. "Well, I'm sure as heck not going to
kiss him back", pointing to my left cheek.

He sighed, pushed off his chair approached
sideways, quickly leaned over,
kissed my cheek, then fell
back

into his chair, arms outstretched,
a chorus of
"Ahhhh"
as the elders drew back in relief
and wonder at the
bravery
of it.

It was a little nothing to me. Yet
why do I still think of it and why
am I only now embarrassed?

Canoeing on the Little
St. Francis River in March

After taking a break from the J-stroke,
and just letting the river take us
at two miles an hour, the clear
water surprises my open fingers
with its iciness. A shock runs
up my back and into my neck,
but I warm in the sun, and look
down to see a forest of watercress
waving its round, green petals
on long stocks. By lacing my fingers
through its leaves, I pull some out
of the stream and hold it outside
the boat, water dripping off
its heavy clumpiness. Someone
drags a towel from below and lays
it on a seat where we settle
the glistening tangle. We each
take a turn sampling peppery
brightness that brings juices
in our mouths. We see
a sleek brown mink, running
in the linear shade
created by the overhang
on the opposite bank.

Finding a New Home

Tired after a flight to her new job
at Blue Dasher Farm, the beekeeper
walks a field of white hair-sheep.
She sees a dark spot in her eye
but it sways in the noon-lit sky.
Larger and larger it gestures
to her question, a low sound
she knows. Willing the swarm to fly
to her, she stops, the spun honey
of her hair waving hello in the air.
She watches a vibrating soccer ball
land on the end of a nearby branch.
Excited, she puts on her safety suit
and finds a cardboard box,
sites it, and with one flick
of the branch, the swarm
falls inside. She sees the queen,
warm at the core, and repositions
the crown of her beekeeper's veil.

And Death, Like a Friend,
Takes You by the Hand

"Get me out of here!", my grandfather cried
from his nursing home bed. And we did.
Brought him home where he sat in his
living room easy chair, (the one that's in
our great room now), where he lay, the
mayfly of his breath fluttering around
his blue-grey sweater.

I sat beside him all afternoon, afraid,
holding his hand while he gathered his
determination to balance the weight
of his fatigue, both pressing on his
fragile ribs. "Betty", he whispered,
"Sometimes life is hard."

He was a gentleman farmer, a lover
of words and their meanings; a
sweet man, adored by his theatrical
wife. He died In their bed a few weeks
later, in the middle of the night, beside
my grandmother who knew it, but who lay
beside him until morning, waiting to call
the undertaker so as not to disturb his
sleep.

Thank you

I am eternally grateful for friends who helped me learn that writing poetry is as satisfying as reading it. Thank you, thank you to Christine Stewart-Nuñez, Darla Biel, Erika Saunders, Bonnie Lievan, Dorianne Paso, and Heather Banks. Special thanks also to my Monday Poetry Roundtable friends: David Allan Evans, Kathie Evans and Dana Yost, who not only have read and critiqued my poems for many years, but who also encouraged me to compile this chapbook.

Betty L Beer has lived in Brookings, SD for 30 years. She is married to Dr. Woody Franklin, a Brookings veterinarian, and has one son, Jake, and two granddaughters. She practiced law in Illinois and was named one of the top ten percent of lawyers in Illinois. She is a Board Member of the South Dakota State Poetry Society, plays the harp and piano, draws and paints, and likes chess.

ACKNOWLEDGMENTS

Many thanks to the editors of the following publications for publishing various poems from this collection:

Oakwood Magazine, 2019, "The Day I Was Beckoned Into a Watercolor"
Pasque Petals, Spring/ Fall 2014, vol. 88:3-4, "Neighbors, 1927"
Pasque Petals, Fall 2019, Vol. 90:5, "Sounds of Mackinac Island, Called Big Turtle"
Pasque Petals, Spring, 2021, vol. 90:8, "The Story of a Drawing"
Pasque Petals, Spring, 2023, vol. 97:1 "Could"
Pasque Petals, Fall, 2023, vol. 97:2, "Skating Match"
Pasque Petals, Spring, 2024, "Calculating Angles", Portrait Contest winner, 3rd place
Pasque Petals, Fall 2024, vol. 98.2, "Shapeshifter"
Pasque Petals, Spring 2025, "Vision Quest"
Perspectives From the Prairie, The Prairie Doc/ Healing Words Foundation, 2023, vol. 1, "Neighbors, 1927"
South Dakota in Poems, 2020, "Neighbors, 1927"
South Dakota Magazine, March/April 2025, "Finding a New Home"

www.ingramcontent.com/pod-product-compliance
Lightning Source LLC
Chambersburg PA
CBHW060136260626

47160CB00005B/2127